The Muddy Princ[ess and]
Spotty The Tortoise

Written by: Sara Quinlan

Illustrated by: Georgie Anderson

For Greta
Love from Nana Sal xx
03.06.2021
:)

For my real Muddy Princess & Big Brother,

Elsie & Isaac

And to the REAL Spotty, thanks for the

inspiration...

The Muddy Princess lived with her Mummy, Daddy and Big Brother. She wasn't really a Princess, she lived in an ordinary home, but her Grandad or "Rah-Rah" always called her a Princess therefore it must have been true!

Muddy
Princess

Rah Rah

Everyday she would wear a pretty dress and her welly boots and 99 bananas out of 100, she would be muddy! She also had a delightful plume of ginger hair upon her head, but this was no ordinary delightful plume of ginger hair, oh my whoospy-daisies, no! It was MAGIC! (but you'll find out about that later...)

The Muddy Princess and her family lived next door to a very old tortoise called Spotty. The Muddy Princess and Spotty loved to have a good old chit-chat over the fence between their gardens. They would talk for hours about all kinds of things like books, gardening, the weather, politics...but their favourite topic of conversation was dandelions!

Spotty was dotty about dandelions, he adored them, he thought they were the most delicious thing in the world! Everyday he would eat them for breakfast, snack, brunch, lunch, afternoon tea, dinner, pudding and supper. The Muddy Princess loved to help her friend by collecting dandelions for him whenever she could.

One sunny morning, the Muddy Princess put on her favourite welly boots and went out for a walk with her Mummy and Big Brother. While on their walk they would usually collect dandelions for Spotty in their special blue dandelion-collecting bucket. Unfortunately, on this particular morning they could not find any dandelions. This made the Muddy Princess feel sad, she couldn't bear the thought of her dear friend Spotty going hungry!

Then she had an idea. She held on to her Big

Brother with one hand and holding the special

blue dandelion-collecting bucket in the other,

she started to shake her MAGIC delightful

plume of ginger hair and

WIZZ, POP, SHAKE, DANDELION CAKE...

The Muddy Princess and her Big Brother found

themselves in the most ginormous field full of

probably a gazillion dandelions!

"Oh my gooseberry gateaux!" shrieked the Muddy Princess, "look at all these dandelions!"

The field was not only full of yellow dandelions, the ones that Spotty liked the best, but also the white wispy ones that you can blow and shake to make all the seeds glide gently away in the breeze.

The Muddy Princess and her Big Brother were thrilled to be filling their special blue dandelion-collecting bucket with lots of yellowy, golden, juicy, delicious Dandelions. They were also blowing and shaking the seeds from the white wispy dandelions to make sure more and more would grow in their place. They really were having the most wonderful time.

All of a sudden they could hear a rumbling sound.

"Was that your tummy rumbling!?" laughed

Big Brother.

"I don't think so..." replied the Muddy Princess "I

ate all of my Bibbix for breakfast this morning".

The rumbling sound started to get louder and

louder, "Oh my dandy daffodils", yelled the Muddy

Princess, "RUN!" A gigantic green tractor with

huge lawn mowers at the back was heading

quickly straight towards them!

They ran and they ran and the Muddy Princess had to think fast. She grabbed her Big Brother by the hand, holding their special blue dandelion-collecting bucket in the other and once again started to shake her MAGIC delightful plume of ginger hair and WIZZ, POP, SHAKE, TAKE-US-BACK-TO-MUMMY CAKE!

The Muddy Princess and her Big Brother landed on

their bottoms in front of Mummy with a thump!

"What are you two up to!?" giggled Mummy. The

Muddy Princess and her Big Brother looked at

each other and then at their special blue

dandelion-collecting bucket. A huge smile spread

across their faces. It was full to the brim of

scrumptious yellow Dandelions!

"Oh my store-bee sundays!" cried the Muddy Princess. The Muddy Princess, her Mummy and Big Brother rushed back home. Once home the Muddy Princess and her Big Brother stood by the fence between the gardens. "Spotty!" they both called out, "look what we've got!". Spotty wandered over to them as quickly as a very old tortoise could, while the Muddy Princess and her Big Brother tipped the enormous bucketful of dandelions over the fence.

Spotty was mesmerised, he had never seen quite so many dandelions! That day the old tortoise had enough for breakfast, snack, brunch, lunch, afternoon tea, dinner, pudding and supper...he even had some left overs which he made into dandelion cakes!

CPSIA information can be obtained
at www.ICGtesting.com
Printed in the USA
BVHW061414180321
602893BV00007B/865